For Mark, Alia and Eilidh with thanks for all the support and inspiration.

Picture Kelpies is an imprint of Floris Books
First published in 2011 by Floris Books
Text © 2011 Chani McBain
Illustrations © 2011 Joanne Nethercott
Chani McBain and Joanne Nethercott assert their right
under the Copyright, Designs and Patent Act 1988 to
be identified as the Author and Illustrator of this Work.
Floris Books, 15 Harrison Gardens, Edinburgh
www.florisbooks.co.uk
The publisher acknowledges subsidy from Creative Scotland
towards the publication of this volume.
British Library CIP Data available
ISBN 978-086315-805-6
Printed in China

Ginger Nut

Chani McBain
and Joanne Nethercott

Calum McGregor came from a ginger family.
Calum's mum and dad had red hair.
Calum's big sister Shona and big brother
Jamie had red hair.

Calum's grandpa had red hair before he went bald,
and he still had a bushy red moustache.
Calum even had a cat called Ginger!

But Calum was just boring blond.

Everyone called Calum's family the Red McGregors, but they always forgot that Calum was a McGregor too.
When they went to Mrs, Findlay's bakery, she gave them special treats. "I've saved my last four gingerbread men for the Red McGregors!"

But she always forgot to save one for Calum.

Calum rushed out of school every Friday
when Emma's mum gave them a lift home.
But sometimes she forgot that there should
be three McGregor children in her car.

Calum was fed up with being the odd one out.
He wanted to be ginger like the rest of his family.
He would have to find a way to make his hair red.

Calum was feeding his pet rabbit when he had a wonderful idea.

"Carrot tops!"

he yelled, startling Bugs. "There must be a reason why redheads are called carrot tops."

BUGS

Calum found a big bag of carrots in the kitchen and started to munch.

In case eating the carrot tops didn't work...

he ate the carrot middles...

and bottoms too.

"Where have all my carrots gone?" said Calum's mum. Calum kept quiet.

"I'll have to make cheese scones for tea instead of your favourite carrot cake, Calum."

Calum groaned.
He was still the only blond McGregor,
and now he had to eat yucky
cheese scones for tea.

The next day Calum was stroking Ginger. Her tail flicked in front of his face like a ginger moustache. Calum had a wonderful idea.

"If I put Ginger on my head, I will look just like Grandpa before he went bald!"

Calum lifted Ginger up.

She was **heavier** than he thought,

and a lot **bigger** than his head.

Calum lost his grip...
Ginger tried to cling on
with her sharp claws.

"Ouch!"

But she crashed to the floor...

shot out the door...

ran down the hall...

and hid under Calum's bed.

Calum was still the only blond McGregor. And now he had a sore head and a very frightened cat.

The next day Calum was drawing a family portrait
when he had a wonderful idea.

"A red felt-tip pen!"

But he had just started to colour
his fringe when the pen stopped
working.

He **scribbled** on some paper but nothing came out.

He gave the pen a little tap but nothing came out.

He gave the pen a *really* **hard** shake...

It went all over the carpet, and on Mum's good couch.
Mum's face went so red that she looked like a tomato.

Calum was still the only blond McGregor. And now he'd
been caught red-handed!

The next day Calum was drinking his favourite fizzy drink when he had a wonderful idea.
"If Irn-Bru can turn my tongue orange, maybe it will turn my hair orange too!"

He gulped down one bottle. Yum.

Halfway through the second bottle his tummy started to gurgle.

Hiccup!

He let out an
Irn-Bru-flavoured hiccup.

Hicccupp!!

The next one was even louder than before.

Hiccccupppp!!!

It was no good. Calum couldn't stop hiccupping. He was still the only blond McGregor (with a bright orange tongue). And his brother Jamie had to give him a real scare to stop his hiccups.

None of Calum's wonderful ideas had worked.
"I might as well face it. I'm going to be
the only blond McGregor forever," he sighed.

The next week Calum's mum
and dad announced that his
uncle and aunt from Australia
were coming to visit.

Calum was very
excited.

"Please, please
let them not
be ginger,"

he wished really hard.

When the buzzer rang on the day of the visit
Calum bolted down the stairs...

...and his heart sank. "You must be Calum," said his aunt. "You look so much like your dad." Calum huffed. Couldn't she see that he was blond?

"It's the McGregor nose," she said. "All the best McGregors have that nose:

your grandpa...

your dad...

your uncle...

you...

...and of course Ellie."
Calum was confused. He had never heard of the "McGregor nose".

Calum was just about to
ask who Ellie was, and
what she was doing with
his nose, when a little
girl peeked out
from behind
his uncle's legs.

"Ellie, come and meet your big cousin Calum," said his aunt.

"Hiya," said Ellie shyly.

But Calum couldn't say anything. He could only smile.

Because his little cousin Ellie had bright blonde hair, just like him.

Calum *still* wasn't ginger, but he did have the same nose as his dad. And now there were two blond McGregors. Maybe there was more to being a McGregor than having ginger hair.